D0820119

CUENTO
DE LUZ

To my daughters, Carlota and Clara.

- María Teresa Barahona -

Text © María Teresa Barahona
Illustrations © Edie Pijpers
This edition © 2014 Cuento de Luz SL
Calle Claveles 10 | Urb Monteclaro | Pozuelo de Alarcón | 28223 | Madrid | Spain
www.cuentodeluz.com
Title in Spanish: ¡Qué divertido es comer frutas!
English translation by Jon Brokenbrow

ISBN: 978-84-16078-32-5

Printed by Shanghai Chenxi Printing Co., Ltd. May 2014, print number 1434-4

All rights reserved

FSC
www.fsc.org
MIX
Paper from
responsible sources
FSC® C007923

Fun and fruit

1jp   10/22/15

FUN AND FRUIT

María Teresa Barahona

Edie Pijpers

In a little town in the south of Spain, next to the sea, lived two little girls named Charlotte and Claire. It was a lovely place, surrounded by magical trees which grew wonderful fruits with thousands of different colors and aromas.

As the girls laughed and skipped on their way to school, they decided to play a game. Every day of the week they would choose a color, think of a fruit in the same color, make up a short story about it, and then eat it for their afternoon snack.

On Monday, they chose yellow.

Charlotte imagined a lemon in the shape of a cloud—a magical cloud that showered raindrops of vitamins on the children so that they would grow strong and healthy.

"Well," said Claire, "I'll tell our cousins Josh and Harry to make me a ball in the shape of an apple, so that the soldiers can play soccer with it and not go to war."

On Tuesday, the color was orange.

Charlotte, who was the oldest, thought, "Oh! I can say a color and a fruit with the same word!
That's funny!"

Claire, who was sitting next to her reading a story, thought about apricots and their soft skin. She would sew them together into a blanket, so that her dog Max wouldn't be cold when they went out walking.

Wednesday arrived, and they both agreed that as Claire was always crashing around and had her legs covered with bruises, the color would be...purple.

Laughing, the little girl shouted, "Plums! Yes, plums! So we can make some yummy jam and Auntie Alice can bake a huge cake for my birthday. We'll organize a pajama party with my friends, and the next morning when we wake up, we can have the whole cake for breakfast."

Charlotte thought about figs, which are very sweet and gave her lots of energy for dancing. Charlie, her sweet-toothed teddy bear, loved them.

On Thursday, they decided the color would be red.

"I always remember," said Charlotte, "that when I was little, I got
a strawberry costume for Christmas at our grandparents' house.
I loved it so much that I wanted to wear it all day long, and even in bed!"

"Well when I was little," said Claire, "Mom always hung cherries on my ears like earrings, and I pretended to be a ballet dancer with a red tutu, dancing in a huge room full of mirrors."

On Friday the color was green, and Charlotte told her sister why pears were her favorite fruit. "When I eat them, I close my eyes and feel little sparkling stars in my mouth that make me dream."

Claire thought about grapes. "They're little, they're always cuddled up close together, and they remind me of the friends I always want to be with," she said.

On Saturday, while walking to the beach, they decided the color would be brown. Straight away, Charlotte decided she would make a lollipop in the shape of a chestnut and give it to her Dad.

"When I'm grown up," said Claire, "I'll be a doctor, and I'll make a boat out of a coconut shell to sail to far-off countries and cure children who are ill, so they can run and jump again."

When they woke up on Sunday, the last day of the game, it was raining, but the sun soon came out and they saw a beautiful rainbow. That gave them an idea—they'd make a rainbow out of fruit, a rainbow you could eat!

That sounds delicious!" said Charlotte, "We'll make a milkshake with banana, tangerines, pears, apples, strawberries, and lots of other fruits. I'll invite my friends to come over and play, and we can all have one for a snack!"

"Yum!" said her sister, "A fruit salad with pieces of watermelon, cantaloupe, apricot, apple, blackberries, strawberries, kiwi fruit and walnuts would be delicious too. I'll imagine it's a big swimming pool where I can swim with our cousins: Josh will be the apple, Harry the cantaloupe, Samuel the strawberry, Jacob the banana, Emily the watermelon, Ethan the peach, Olivia the orange, and I'll be the tangerine. I'll invite my sister Charlotte too, who can be the pear, so she knows that even though we get angry with each other every now and then, I LOVE HER LOTS AND LOTS!" And with a wink she added, "And I'm sure she loves me too!"

And so, as they played, the two sisters realized what a great time they had together, and how healthy and fun it was to eat fruit every day.